D1643662

Babbity's BIG Bad Mood

M Christina Butler

Illustrated by Frank Endersby

LITTLE TIGER PRESS
London

Babbity Rabbit woke up one morning
feeling very grumpy. The sun was shining
and the birds were singing, but Babbity
was in a big bad mood!

"Bother those noisy birds!" he muttered.
"And bother the sun as well!"

Babbity sat on a branch and felt cross.
"Hello!" cried Squirrel and Mouse,
scampering up. "Are you ready for
our picnic?"

"Harrumph," mumbled Babbity,
and stuck out his bottom lip.
    "Oh dear!" said Squirrel. "Where's
your bad mood come from?"
    "I don't know," Babbity grumbled.
"It was there when I got out of bed."

"Look, Babbity," laughed Mouse, trying to cheer him up with a clever trick. Babbity wasn't impressed.

"What about this?" Squirrel cried, turning head over heels.

It's not *fair*! Babbity thought.
My feet are too big for that.
And he stomped off up the hill.

"Let's do what Babbity does,"
Mouse whispered to Squirrel.
"It might make him laugh."

So they stamped their feet and looked as cross as they could. But Babbity didn't even notice.

"We've found the top of the world!" Squirrel cried when they reached the hilltop.

"Look, Babbity," called Mouse. "We can see for miles and miles!"

But a bumblebee
buzzed around
Babbity's nose.

"Bother that bee!"
he huffed.

"Buzz off, Bumble!"

"I know a good game," said Squirrel, stretching out on the grass. "We pick a cloud and see if it looks like something."

"I can see a rabbit," cried Mouse, "and it looks just like Babbity!"

Babbity stared at the cloud. It had two rabbit ears and a big, grumpy face!

"It doesn't look a *bit* like me!"
he sulked, and he closed his
eyes tight so he couldn't see
the cloud any more.

"Right," said Squirrel standing up, "I know what will cheer you up – let's all do handstands!"

"No thanks," Babbity muttered.

"Oh come on, Babbity," said Mouse. "Don't be such a spoilsport."

"I don't want to play your stupid games!" Babbity snapped, and stormed off by himself.

Babbity sat all alone
feeling grumpy and sad . . .

while Squirrel and Mouse
played together in the sunshine.

A ladybird was sunbathing nearby, when it fell on its back and couldn't get up.

"Are you having a bad day too?" Babbity said, gently turning it over.

The ladybird hummed as it flew away. Babbity started to smile.

"Let's all roll to the bottom of the
hill!" said Mouse, bounding over.
"All right," said Babbity, quietly.

With their heads in a spin and their legs in a twirl, they went bumbling and bouncing all the way down, twisting and turning through the long grass.

"That was *brilliant!*" Babbity laughed happily.

"Hey, Babbity," said Squirrel, "your bad mood has gone! Where do you think it could be?"

"I don't know," he chuckled. "Perhaps I left it on top of the hill!"

Then looking round he said, "Where's Mouse?"

Babbity and Squirrel found Mouse
half way up the bank, stuck in
a molehill.
"Are you all right?" asked Babbity.

"Bother that stupid molehill!" sniffed Mouse, brushing down her fur.

"Oh dear," Squirrel whispered, "now *Mouse* is feeling grumpy."

"Don't worry," said Babbity, "together we'll get rid of that bad mood for good!"

And Babbity and Squirrel gave Mouse a great big hug.